Pelican Rescue

Story by Rose Inserra
Illustrations by Francesca Rosa

Contents

Chapter 1

A Special Find at Salty Point Beach

"Blake! Holly!" Dad called out. "Be careful. There is so much seaweed on the beach. There might be something sharp."

It was Holly and Blake's first time at Salty Point Beach. Dad had just moved to a new house a little way up the road.

Blake slowed down and began to walk. "Okay, Dad!" he said, but Holly ran ahead.

"Stop, Holly!" said Blake. "I can see a fishing hook on a piece of tangled line."

Holly stopped just in time. She could see a sharp hook on some fishing line, tied around a plastic water bottle.

"Dad, why is this beach so full of rubbish and seaweed?" she asked.

"There was a storm last night, and the rubbish has all washed up on the shore," Dad said.

"How does it get in the water?" Blake wanted to know.

"People throw their rubbish away near waterways and on the beach. It collects in the storm water drains, then washes out to sea. Later, the tide brings it back to the shore," Dad explained.

"Look at that big brown lump of plastic near the jetty," said Holly, pointing to a large lumpy shape.

As Holly, Blake and Dad approached it, the lumpy shape moved.

"What is it?" asked Holly, feeling a little worried.

"It's a big bird," said Blake. "I can see it's got a really big bill."

"Dad, it's a pelican!" cried Holly.

The pelican was dirty and covered in wet sand. There was tangled fishing line wrapped around its feet and over its wings.

"The poor pelican! It's all tangled in the fishing line," said Holly.

"And it won't be able to catch fish or fly," added Blake.

"We need to get some help, Dad," said Blake and Holly together.

Chapter 2

Help from the Seabird Rescue Team

A man who had been fishing from the jetty came over.

"Hello. I'm Pete," he said. "I've already called the seabird rescue team. They should be here soon."

"Do many animals get caught in rubbish?" asked Blake.

"Sadly, yes," said Pete. "When you go fishing, it's important not to throw away your old line, especially if it's got hooks on it. The birds get tangled in it and they can get injured."

"How do pelicans get injured by hooks?" Holly asked.

Pete explained, "Pelicans love to eat fish, so they hang around the places where people go fishing. That's the trouble. The fishing hooks can tear their bills and their bill pouches, or pelicans can swallow the hooks and damage their insides."

"What's a bill pouch?" asked Blake.

"Can you see that skin hanging down from the pelican's bill?" said Pete, pointing to the injured pelican. "That's a pouch. It's used to scoop up fish from the water."

"What can we do to help the pelican?" Holly asked.

"We need to keep very quiet and still," said Pete, "so we don't scare it."

Just then, two people from the seabird rescue team arrived in a van. They carried a large container lined with blankets and towels.

"Hello, everyone. I'm Lisa and this is Cathy," said one of the rescuers.

They both went over to look at the injured pelican.

"Pelly here has been rescued before," said Cathy. "See the band around his leg? We know this pelican is a male. We put that leg band on him last time, so we could track him. His number is P-651."

"Is Pelly his name?" asked Holly.

"Well, not really," Cathy said. "We call every pelican we rescue 'Pelly'."

"Now," Lisa said, "everyone will need to move away from the pelican so we can catch him and put him in the container."

Lisa and Cathy approached Pelly slowly.
Then Lisa quickly and firmly wrapped her arms around him.

She held Pelly's bill so he couldn't move it around.

Pelly tried to get away, but Cathy and Lisa quickly moved him inside the container.

"We need to get him to our seabird rescue centre.
The vet will check him there," said Lisa.

"Why don't you come down to the rescue centre tomorrow and check on Pelly?" asked Cathy.

"Can we? Please Dad," begged Blake and Holly.

"Yes. I think Pelly will like that," said Dad.

Chapter 3

Visiting Pelly

The next day, Holly and Blake woke up early.

"Hurry, Dad. Let's go and visit Pelly at the seabird rescue centre," Blake said.

Both Blake and Holly felt a little worried. What if Pelly wasn't all right?

But they didn't have to worry. When they got to the rescue centre, they quickly spotted Pelly in the corner of the room.

Holly and Blake found Cathy and Lisa.

"Is Pelly going to be okay?" asked Blake.

"The vet has checked him, and he only has a few cuts from the fishing line," Lisa told them. "He will be okay if we can get him to drink and eat again."

"What about this other pelican?" Holly asked, pointing to a smaller pelican.

"Well, *that* Pelly tore her bill pouch on a fish hook and she has a cut on her wing. She needs to have stitches," Cathy said. "She will have to stay here for a while longer."

Holly and Blake looked around the rescue centre.
There were lots of other seabirds – and all of them needed care.

They gave each other worried looks.

"We all need to be careful about how much plastic and other rubbish is thrown out into the ocean," said Lisa. "Here, let me show you something."

Lisa opened her laptop and looked up a website. "There is an island of rubbish in the Pacific Ocean called the Great Pacific Garbage Patch," she said.

"What sort of island is it?" Blake asked.

Lisa explained, "It's just a whole lot of rubbish, like straws and other plastic waste, that has joined together to make an island. This rubbish and other plastic waste stays in the ocean for years and years. Sometimes only tiny pieces are left."

"Then, the marine animals that live there feed on the plastic and it makes them get sick or die," Lisa added. "Others get tangled in bits of plastic and fishing nets."

"Maybe we can do something to help get rid of the rubbish at Salty Point Beach," said Holly.

"Yes. We should do something," said Blake, wishing he could help Pelly and the other seabirds.

At dinner time, Holly and Blake talked to Dad about the problem of ocean rubbish.

"Dad, do you think we could start by doing a clean-up on the beach next weekend?" asked Blake.

"We can give it a try," said Dad.

Chapter 4

Bins on the Beach

The next weekend, Blake, Holly and Dad spent the whole day picking up rubbish on Salty Point Beach.

By the middle of the afternoon, the big bins were full, and the beach nearby was clean. They felt very tired.

Holly, Dad and Blake looked over at the rubbish on the far side of the jetty. But there was no more room in the bins to put the rubbish in.

"This beach needs more bins," said Holly.

"I know some other beaches have special bins for hooks and fishing line," said Dad.

"Can we send the council an email and ask if they can put the special bins at Salty Point Beach?" asked Blake.

"That's a good idea. Dad, can we go home and send an email now?" asked Holly.

Two weeks later, Holly and Blake arrived back at Dad's house. The first thing they did was go down to the beach.

"Look!" said Blake, feeling excited. "There are special bins for hooks and fishing line!"

"And there's no rubbish on the beach!" said Holly.

"Yes, the council agreed to the special bins," said Dad, smiling.

Just then, Holly spotted a van pulling into the parking area.

"Dad, isn't that Cathy and Lisa's van?" she said.

Blake and Holly ran over to the van, just as Cathy and Lisa were lifting a pelican out of a container and placing it gently on the sand. It was Pelly! His feathers were nice and clean, his feet were healed, and he looked healthy.

After taking a few steps, Pelly opened his wings.
He was ready to fly again.

Holly and Blake gave each other a high five as they watched the pelican's large wings lift, and he took off high into the air.

Chapter 5

A Pelican Family

During the school holidays, Blake and Holly stayed at Dad's place.

"I wonder if Pelly's back at the jetty," called Holly, as she and Blake raced towards the beach.

A large pelican was perched on a post at the jetty. On the jetty below it were two smaller pelicans.

"It's not Pelly. It's too big," said Blake.

"Maybe he's been eating lots of fish," said Dad.

As they got closer, they could see the large letters on the band on the pelican's leg.

"It *is* Pelly!" shouted Holly. "And he's brought his family."

"The Pelly family!" said Blake, laughing.

"A family – just like us," replied Holly.